The Case of
Maker Mischief

For Mom and Tony, who taught me
to love a good book — *Liam*

To my favorite misfits — *Aurélie*

West Meadows Detectives

The Case of Maker Mischief

Written by
Liam O'Donnell

Illustrated by
Aurélie Grand

Owlkids Books

Owlkids Books acknowledges the financial support of the Canada Council for the
Arts, the Ontario Arts Council, the Government of Canada through the Canada
Book Fund (CBF) and the Government of Ontario through the Ontario Creates
Book Initiative for our publishing activities.

Published in Canada by
Owlkids Books Inc.
1 Eglinton Avenue East
Toronto, ON M4P 3A1

Published in the United States by
Owlkids Books Inc.
1700 Fourth Street
Berkeley, CA 94710

Cataloguing data available from Library and Archives Canada

ISBN 978-1-77147-070-4 (hardcover)
ISBN 978-1-77147-385-9 (softcover)

Library of Congress Control Number: 2016930940

Edited by Debbie Rogosin
Designed by Claudia Dávila

ONTARIO ARTS COUNCIL
CONSEIL DES ARTS DE L'ONTARIO
an Ontario government agency
un organisme du gouvernement de l'Ontario

Canada Council
for the Arts

Conseil des Arts
du Canada

Canada

Manufactured in Altona, MB, Canada, in April 2019, by Friesens Corporation
Job #251392

B   C   D   E   F   G

Publisher of Chirp, Chickadee and OWL
www.owlkidsbooks.com

Owlkids Books is a division of  bayard canada

Table of Contents

CHAPTER 1

The doorbell rang at 7:49 on Friday morning.

That was the first clue something was wrong. Nobody should be coming to our front door at that time. Friday mornings are when people get ready for school or work.

Downstairs, I heard my mom open the door and speak to someone.

"Myron," she called from the bottom of the stairs. "You have a visitor."

"I'm not supposed to have visitors," I called back. I sat on my bed and put a sock on my left foot. "I'm supposed to be getting ready for school."

"I know, dear," Mom called. "I don't want to upset your routine, but he insists he speak with you."

Routines are important to me. When I do the same thing at the same time every day, I feel calm. Unexpected things do not make me feel calm. And someone ringing the doorbell at 7:49 in the morning was very unexpected.

In the kitchen, my baby sister, Sofia, cried in her high chair. She was waiting for her breakfast. That was her morning routine. She wasn't happy about this unexpected visitor either.

"Myron, please come down." Mom used her singsong voice. That's how she speaks when she wants me to do something I really don't want to do. "He says he's a friend from school."

I paused with a sock halfway on my right foot. A friend from school? I'd just started at West Meadows Elementary last month. I didn't have many friends there. That meant the list of suspects was small. Now I was curious. A good detective is always curious.

I pulled on my sock and went downstairs.

Jordan stood inside our front door. He was in my morning class at school, so he was on my suspect list. But that didn't explain why he was at my house before school. Sofia screamed louder from the other room.

"I'll let you talk with your friend," Mom said. She went back into the kitchen.

Jordan wiped his nose with his sleeve. He had short black hair that stuck straight out just above his left ear. He looked like he had just woken up. His eyes were red and swollen, too. He had either been crying or had allergies. It was the middle of October, so I didn't think it was allergies. That meant he had been crying.

"Why are you here?" I said.

"I didn't want to miss you," he sniffed.

"How could you miss me?" I said. "We're in the same class. Our class has four people in it. Five if you count Mr. Harpel. And I would, since he's our teacher. But that doesn't answer my question. Why are you here?"

"Someone stole Robson," Jordan said in a low voice.

"Robson...your robot?"

Jordan nodded. His appearance on my doorstep suddenly made sense.

I had a new mystery to solve.

Fifteen minutes later, I was lost.

"This isn't the way to school," I said. "We've been walking for seven minutes and we're still not at school. We're going to be late."

"We're taking a detour." Jordan hurried down the sidewalk.

He had not stopped walking since I agreed to find Robson the Robot. Jordan had paced in a tight circle in our front hallway while I got ready. Now he balled his hands into fists as he walked. I knew that meant he was really upset. I'm not good at guessing how people feel, but with Jordan, it's not too hard. When he makes a fist, he's mad. That's when he hits things or people. He always apologizes after, but when he gets mad, he loses control.

Control is important to me, too. When things get out of control, my brain itches and I want to disappear. Finding Jordan's robot would help Jordan get control back. That's why I agreed to change my morning routine. I ate a banana for breakfast instead of having a bowl of apple and cinnamon oatmeal.

I opened my detective notebook to a blank page, pulled a fresh black pen from my pocket, and asked Jordan to tell me about the robot theft from the beginning.

"Robson is the robot I'm building with Glitch for the Robot Maze Challenge at the Maker Faire," Jordan explained. Glitch is in our morning class, too. Her real name is Danielle, but everyone calls her Glitch because she knows a lot about computers. "The Maker Faire is happening in Oakdale Park this weekend. It's for people who like to build stuff and see how stuff works."

"Like robots?" I asked. I hurried to keep up with Jordan. My notes were messy. Writing while walking is a detective skill I needed to work on.

"Robots, mini-computers, and other cool stuff," Jordan said. "Glitch and I have been building our robot in Ms. Fay's after-school Maker Club in the library. I'm doing the design, and Glitch is writing all the computer code that makes the bot move."

"I've seen the plans for your robot on your desk," I said.

"That's the other thing," Jordan said. "I can't find those plans. I searched for them yesterday, but they've vanished."

"That's impossible," I said. "Things don't vanish, Jordan."

"I know! That's why I'm sure it's all connected."

"Connected to what?" I asked.

"We finished the bot yesterday," he said. "I brought it home to add details to the paint job. I put it in the shed in our backyard. When I went to check on it this morning, it was gone."

Jordan followed the sidewalk around a corner and stopped. We stood at the top of a tree-lined street.

"My house is at the end of this street," Jordan said.

My brain began to itch.

"We don't have time to go to your house," I said. "We'll be late for school. I'm never late."

"Relax, Myron. We're not going to my house." Jordon pointed to a small redbrick house across the road. "We're going there."

It was the first house on the street. There was a gnome made of stone sitting at an angle near the cracked cement steps. The gnome was cracked, too.

"We don't have time to go there either," I said.

"Yes we do."

Jordan took my arm and pulled me along as he marched across the street. He knocked loudly on the door.

"Who lives here?" I said.

The door opened and I got my answer.

Smasher McGintley, the biggest bully at West Meadows Elementary, stood in the doorway. Half a piece of toast hung from her mouth.

"What are you two doing here?" She tore off a chunk of toast and chomped it as she glared at us. I suddenly remembered the T. rex exhibit at the museum and was glad I had stopped in the bathroom before we left my house.

"We know you took my robot, Smasher." Jordan's hands were curled into fists again.

I was scared he was going to hit her. Instead, he pushed me closer to Smasher. "And I've hired the best detective in town to get it back. Meet Myron Matthews."

"I know Myron the Snoop," Smasher snarled. "We go to the same school, remember? Now go away. I didn't steal your dumb robot."

"Yes you did." Jordan wasn't backing down. "You even said so."

Smasher stopped chewing. "What are you talking about?"

"At last week's Maker Club meeting, you said you liked our robot so much, you were going to take it for yourself."

"I was joking," Smasher said.

"And now you're lying." Jordan put his hand on my shoulder. "Myron Matthews is going to bring you down, Smasher!"

"Is he, now?" Smasher loomed over me. "And what does the great detective have to say about that?"

My throat closed. Breathing suddenly became very difficult. Smasher took another bite of toast and grinned as she chewed it into mush. If we stood here much longer, we would be mush, too.

A blue van stopped at the corner of the street and honked. There was a commotion inside and I could see someone clambering into the front. Then Hajrah, my detective

partner, stuck her head out the van's passenger side window.

"Myron and

Jordan! I knew it was you guys," Hajrah shouted. "My mom didn't believe me. But I was right again!" Hajrah spotted Smasher and frowned. "Is everything okay? Do you need a ride to school?"

"Yes, we do," I said, suddenly able to speak again. "Good-bye, Smasher."

I hurried away from the house, pulling Jordan with me.

"This isn't over, Smasher!" Jordan shouted.

"You're right," Smasher called back. "The fun is just beginning."

We scrambled into the van. Hajrah's mom drove away with surprising speed.

Hajrah turned to me. Her long black braid whipped around with her and rested over her shoulder.

"Good thing we were passing by. Smasher

did *not* look happy to see you."

"True," I said. "But I'm very happy to see you!"

When I first moved to West Meadows, I didn't want a detective partner. Now, I don't know how I survived without one.

CHAPTER 2

The van arrived at school. We hopped out and thanked Hajrah's mom for the ride. As soon as she pulled away from the curb, Hajrah grabbed my sleeve.

"Okay, what's going on?" she said. "Why were you at Smasher's house?"

She bounced on her toes in front of us, waiting for an answer. Hajrah is good at knowing when someone isn't telling the truth. But she's never good at being still.

"Myron is going to prove Smasher stole Robson the Robot," Jordan said.

"We have a new case? Awesome!" Hajrah swung her backpack around in a wide circle. The school bell rang. "Tell me about it inside." She ran into the school, still swinging her backpack.

There was a mouse in room 15. It rolled across the carpet and stopped at my feet. It wasn't a real mouse. It was a robot. It had wheels, wires, and a wifi connection to the Internet. It also had Mr. Harpel's voice.

"Good morning, Myron and company!" The words came from two tiny speakers in the mouse's ears and the voice sounded exactly like my teacher's.

"Mousebot!" Hajrah squealed.

Jordan's face lit up. "You're working again!"

Hajrah dropped to her knees and got nose to nose with the robot mouse.

"Did Glitch fix you, little mousie?"

"Yes I did," Glitch said from the far side of the room. She had Mousebot's remote control in her hands.

The robot mouse was one of the first bots Glitch built. She made it during the summer and brought it into class a few weeks ago. It didn't look like a mouse at first. Then Jordan had an idea. He made a mouse-shaped body out of cardboard to hide its wires.

The real Mr. Harpel bustled into the room. "Good morning, Myron and company!"

"You said that twice. But the first time, it

was a recording of your voice on Mousebot."

Mr. Harpel stopped and turned. He was tall and round, with a bushy beard. He was kind and funny and sometimes didn't act like a teacher at all. He laughed from his belly and wore shoes with no laces. I liked shoes with no laces.

"So I did, Myron," he said, looking at Mousebot and chuckling. "Very observant."

Mousebot zipped around in a tight circle in the middle of the carpet.

"Good morning, Myron! Hello, Hajrah! Good morning, Myron! Hello, Hajrah!" Mousebot repeated until everyone was laughing.

Room 15 was a different kind of classroom. There were only four students in our class, and we each had our own space that we

didn't have to share. My space was against
the far wall, next to a tall bookshelf filled
with books. I had a table and a comfortable
chair that was perfect for reading really good
mysteries. Being in room 15 always calmed
me when my brain got too itchy.

Mr. Harpel called us all to the carpet for
our morning meeting. The carpet had red
and yellow circles. I always sat in the yellow
circle near my table. Glitch put Mousebot
away on her desk and sat on the carpet
without a word. Jordan sat down beside her.
The smiles and laughter from a few minutes
ago were gone.

Mr. Harpel looked around the room and
frowned. "What happened? Why is everyone
so glum now?"

"I'm not glum!" Hajrah belly flopped onto

her yoga ball and balanced as if she were flying. She only lasted a few seconds before falling off. "I don't even know what it means, but I don't think I'm it."

"Glum means sad," I said. I turned to Mr. Harpel. "Glitch and Jordan are glum because there's been a theft."

"A theft? Here at school?" Mr. Harpel said.

Jordan shook his head. "From my shed."

"I'm sorry to hear that." Mr. Harpel sat in his chair near the front of the room. "Do you want to talk about it?"

They did. Jordan and Glitch told Mr. Harpel and Hajrah everything about their robot and the upcoming competition at the Maker Faire.

"Why do you think Smasher took your robot?" Hajrah asked when they were finished.

"Because Smasher takes everything," Glitch said. "Ms. Fay brings in stuff like lights and buzzers for us to add to our projects."

"Smasher always takes the best pieces from everybody," Jordan added.

"Have you told Ms. Fay?" Mr. Harpel asked. "I'm sure she would help you get them back. That might be a good way to solve the problem."

"It's also a good way to get a fat lip," Jordan mumbled. "Telling a teacher about Smasher just leads to bigger problems."

I knew exactly what Jordan meant. Smasher McGintley ruled the schoolyard. Even the older kids stayed clear of her.

"I'll talk to Ms. Fay and ask her to keep an eye on Smasher during the Maker Club meetings," Mr. Harpel said.

"Could you ask her to make Smasher return our bot?" Glitch said.

"We don't know Smasher took Robson," I said.

Jordan's hands became fists again. "At the last club meeting, she said she wanted to take it."

"She told us it was a joke," I said. "If I'm going to catch the thief, we need hard evidence. We need to catch the thief *with* Robson the Robot."

"That's why I took you to Smasher's house this morning!"

"All she had was a piece of toast," I said.

"And if I hadn't shown up, she would have had your heads, too." Hajrah jumped to her feet and bowed. "But you don't have to thank me. I'm always happy to save the day."

Mr. Harpel and I chuckled. Even Jordan grinned.

Glitch didn't smile. "Finding the robot won't be easy." She went to the whiteboard and uncapped a green dry-erase marker. "Our robot is made up of three parts." She drew two rectangles on the board. "First there is the robot case. It's made of plastic. Jordan put it together and painted it. The second part is the hardware inside the robot case."

"That's all the motors and sensors that make it move," Jordan explained. "Ms. Fay gave us the pieces and helped us put them together."

"The third part is the computer code that makes the bot move. Ms. Fay helped with that, too." Glitch drew another shape on the board. She put a big circle around all three parts. "Together, all three pieces make the robot work."

"The thief won't keep the parts together for long," I said. "If they want to use Robson in the maze competition, they'll have to disguise the robot."

"Oh, disguises! I love disguises," Hajrah said. "Wait. How do you disguise a robot?"

"The simplest way is to get rid of the case," Glitch said. "It's easy to pop it off. After that,

each robot would look more or less the same."

"Our robot is about as big as a tissue box and looks like a monster truck." Jordan took a red dry-erase marker and added details to the first box Glitch had drawn. "It has four fat wheels and two sensors at the front that look like headlamps." Jordan added lines along the side of the box. "I painted flames and skulls on it to make it look scary."

"I think it looks cute," Hajrah said.

Jordan frowned. "It's not supposed to be cute."

"Cute or scary, we don't have much time," I said. "We need to find the thief before they take off the case."

Jordan paced the carpet. "Now do you see why I brought you to Smasher's house, Myron?"

"I do, but I still don't appreciate nearly getting smushed so early in the morning."

"I'm sure that wasn't Jordan's intention," Mr. Harpel said. "I'll be helping Ms. Fay at the Maker Faire, so I'll watch out for the missing robot." He looked at me. "In the meantime, it looks like you have some investigating to do, Mr. Detective."

Hajrah planted her feet on the carpet. "And what about Ms. Detective?"

Mr. Harpel laughed. "Of course, Hajrah, how could I forget? You are both detectives."

"We're the West Meadows detectives! We'll solve this mystery." Hajrah turned to me. "And I know where we're going to start our investigation."

"You do?" I said.

Hajrah grinned. "I think it's time to visit the maker space in the library."

CHAPTER 3

The library was busy and loud. Two things I don't like. Especially in a library. But that's what you get when you go there during morning recess.

Every class gets library time once a week. Ms. Fay, the librarian, reads us stories and lets us take out books. If you want to get another book before your class's next library time, you have to go during morning recess. That's the only other time Ms. Fay lets kids return books and take out new ones. That means the library is very busy every morning recess.

I only like visiting the library during our class's library times. Then it's just the kids from room 15 and Mr. Harpel. Even with Hajrah running around shouting out book titles, it's quieter than at recess.

I stopped just outside the library doors.

"I can't go in there," I said.

"I know it's loud, Myron," Hajrah said. "But we need to investigate the maker space before the thief has a chance to remove any evidence."

"It's not just the noise," I said. "It's this." I held up a library book with two kittens on the cover.

"*Baby Animals from around the World*," Hajrah said, reading the title aloud. "It's a great book!"

"It's *your* book."

"And it's *our* cover story, remember?"

"It's not a good cover story," I said. "No one will believe that I took out a book on baby animals. And I am not good at pretending. I always do it wrong."

"Relax, Myron." Hajrah sighed. "No one will care what book you have. And Ms. Fay doesn't let kids come here during recess unless they have a book to return."

"I just wish you had let me choose a better book."

"All your library books are at home. Think of it as a disguise. Detectives disguise themselves all the time. We are disguising ourselves as two kids returning their library books."

"It's not a very good disguise," I said. "Disguises have mustaches and fake noses."

"Well, we have library books," Hajrah snapped. "Just go with it, okay?"

She turned and marched into the library.

I gripped the kitten book so tightly, my knuckles hurt. "Just going with it" is not easy for autistics like me. My brain works differently from other people's brains. And pretending to like books on cats was making my brain buzz.

I followed Hajrah into the library. The buzzing spread down my body to my feet.

I couldn't take another step. Kids pushed past me, dropped their books in the return bin, and ran off in search of new ones. They made it look so easy. Everything came easy to other people, including Hajrah.

I closed my eyes and took a deep breath. It didn't help. I felt a tug on my fingers and cracked my eyes open. Hajrah was standing beside me. She took my hand in hers.

"Come on, detective," she whispered. "We can do this."

"Just going with it" was a lot easier with a friend at your side.

Ms. Fay stood near the book-return bin. She smiled when she saw us. "Myron! I'm surprised to see you here during recess."

"Myron is full of surprises." Hajrah jumped the last few steps to the book-return bin, pulling me along behind her.

We dropped our books in the bin. Ms. Fay frowned when she saw my book.

"*Baby Animals*, Myron?" she said. "I thought you only liked mysteries."

Three things happened at once. The library got very hot. My mouth got very dry. And I very much wanted to run away.

"Myron is expanding his interests," Hajrah said with a wide smile. "It's something Mr. Harpel has been teaching us. In fact, Myron wants another book on baby animals. They're at the back of the library, near the maker space, aren't they?"

"Yes, they are," Ms. Fay said. "Glad to hear you're branching out, Myron!"

Hajrah dragged me to the back of the library as fast as she could.

"Nicely done, detective. She didn't suspect a thing," she whispered.

"That's because I didn't say a thing."

"Exactly!"

The library was quieter back in the nonfiction section. A few older kids were looking at books on ancient civilizations, but they didn't notice us.

The maker space was behind the bookshelves. Right now it was dark and deserted. Six long tables were pushed together, with a big open area in the middle. A large sign read "Maker space closed—Do not enter." That didn't matter to Hajrah. She scurried under one of the tables and popped up in the middle of the maker space.

"Hurry up, Myron!" she hissed.

I scurried under the table, too.

Everybody's work area was labeled with their names, which were taped on top of the tables. Screwdrivers, hammers, and other tools sat on the tabletops. Jordan's and Glitch's areas were beside each other. Next to them was Lionel Aram's work area. He was in my afternoon class with Ms. Chu. A half-built remote-control car with thick wheels lay in pieces on Lionel's table. If he was competing in this weekend's tournament, he had some work to do.

Smasher's work area was a mess. Her tools lay in a heap. Screws and gears and tangles of colorful wires were scattered about. A sour odor wafted up from the table.

"Why does it smell like gym socks?" I stepped back and plugged my nose.

Hajrah covered her face and leaned in close

to the table. "Because there's a half-eaten sandwich under those wires."

"That's disgusting," I said. "Smasher is not a maker. There's no project on her table. Just her unfinished lunch."

Hajrah stepped away from Smasher's work area. "Maybe she took her bot home, like Jordan did."

"Not Smasher," I said. "Not if she's a true McGintley."

"That's right. You knew her cousin from your old neighborhood."

"Yes, I did. Basher McGintley would avoid doing anything if he could get someone else to do it for him."

"And that's what Smasher is doing?"

I nodded. "Even *I* can tell she isn't making anything. She's trying to look busy while someone else builds her a robot."

"Or she steals one," Hajrah said.

"Myron? Hajrah? Recess is nearly over," Ms. Fay called. "Did you find a new book?"

"We're out of time," Hajrah said. She slid under a table and out of the maker space.

"I'm here, Ms. Fay." Hajrah grabbed a book and pretended to be reading it.

"Indoor voices, please, Hajrah," Ms. Fay said.

I dived under a table and crawled to the edge of the maker space. My plan was to pop up behind Ms. Fay and Hajrah. But I didn't pop. I stopped. Something was taped to the underside of one of the tables. It was a piece of paper. I pulled it free.

Lines on the paper formed a box and circles. Arrows showed how the shapes all fit together. Across the top it read "Robson the

Robot, by Jordan and
Glitch." It was Jordan's
missing robot plans!

Whoever stole them
must have hidden
them under their
table. I scrambled
out and checked. The
work area was labeled
"Lionel Aram."

I had found more than the missing robot
plans. I had found another suspect.

CHAPTER 4

"He's gone home, kiddos!" Ms. Levron smacked her chewing gum. "He said he was feeling sick. Poor thing."

Ms. Levron was in charge of the office at school. She gave kids ice when they scraped their knees, and helped Principal Rainer run the school. She had a tattoo of a purple flower on her left shoulder, and she always chewed gum. Gum is not allowed in school. I don't know about tattoos.

We had spent all of our lunch hour looking

for Lionel. We should have come here first.

Hajrah pushed her braid off her shoulder and smiled at Ms. Levron. She held up Jordan's robot plans. "Lionel left some work at his table and we want to let him know we found it," she said. "Can we call him at home?"

She stepped on my right foot when I opened my mouth to correct her.

Ms. Levron's jaw moved up and down three times as she chewed her gum. Her blue eyes darted to me and then back to Hajrah. I couldn't look Ms. Levron in the eye. She would know we weren't telling the whole truth. I focused on the purple flower on her shoulder.

She matched Hajrah's smile with her own. "Sure thing."

She found Lionel's phone number on her

computer and dialed it. She handed Hajrah the phone and went back to stapling a large stack of papers.

Hajrah winked at me as she waited for someone to answer. I was not in the mood for winking.

"This wasn't part of the plan," I hissed. "We should have discussed it first."

She turned her back to me. That meant she didn't want to listen to me. Someone must have answered at Lionel's because Hajrah began speaking so quietly I could not make out what she was saying.

I opened my notebook while I waited and wrote the words "sick—went home" beside Lionel's name. Lionel and Smasher were our two main suspects. Smasher had said she would take Robson the Robot. And it looked like Lionel had taken the plans. Either suspect could be guilty, but we needed more evidence to be certain.

Hajrah hung up the phone.

"His grandfather says Lionel came home about half an hour ago," she said. "He's sleeping and couldn't come to the phone."

I closed my notebook. "So our newest suspect is too sick to talk."

Hajrah tugged on her braid. "But was he too sick to steal?"

The shed in Jordan's backyard looked like a robot graveyard.

Wires, lights, and tools were scattered across the chipped wooden work surface. I crowded into the shed with Jordan, Glitch, and Hajrah. School had finished an hour ago. Jordan and Glitch were happy we'd found their robot plans. Now we were investigating the scene of the crime.

Jordan pointed to an empty space on the table. "I left our robot right there last night. This morning, Robson was gone."

Hajrah stared at the spot with her eyes narrowed. Suddenly, she spun around to face Jordan. "What did you do after you discovered the robot was missing, Mr. Lin?" She spoke in a serious police-detective voice.

"You don't have to call him Mr. Lin," I said.

She rolled her eyes. "It's his last name, Myron. It's how detectives ask questions on TV."

"We're not on TV," I said. "We're in a shed."

"I know, but wouldn't it be cool if we were

on TV?" Hajrah grinned.

"If you two are finished arguing," Jordan interrupted, "I can answer your question."

"We weren't arguing," we both said at the same time.

"Yes you were." Glitch laughed. "You guys do it all the time."

"Anyway," Jordan said, "to answer your question, I checked on the robot this morning before school. When I saw it was gone, I grabbed my stuff and ran straight to Myron's house. First the plans go missing, and then the robot gets stolen. It had to be Smasher, and I knew Myron could prove it."

"Lionel is a suspect, too," I reminded him. "Do you have any idea why he had the plans for your bot taped to his table at the maker space?"

"No idea," Glitch said.

"His robot was a disaster," Jordan said. "The wires were a mess, and his computer code didn't work."

"He wanted me to help him," Glitch said. "But I didn't have time. I had to finish Robson."

"He was pretty mad at us for not helping," Jordan said. "He called us some names I won't repeat."

"Too bad he's too sick to talk to us," I said.

"That's weird," Glitch said. "I saw Lionel leaving school at lunch today. He didn't look sick to me."

Hajrah turned to me. "We totally have to talk to Lionel if we're going to solve this case."

"Agreed." I flipped through my notebook to my suspects page. Under Lionel's name,

I changed my note so it read *"Pretended* to be sick—went home." If Lionel would fake being sick, what else would he lie about?

Hajrah studied the shed's only window. It was covered in thick grime.

"How did the thief get into the shed?" she asked.

"Not through that window. It's painted shut and hasn't opened for years," Jordan said. "The only way in is through the door. And I know I locked it last night."

I ran my hand along the doorframe. There were no scratch marks around the lock.

"Whoever got in used a key," I said.

"Only Dad and I have keys." Jordan held up a key chain. It had a fancy letter "J" on it, and three keys. "No one else comes in here. My mom hates this shed. It creeps her out."

"Only one door, and the window is painted shut," Hajrah said. "The thief is either a ghost or a mouse."

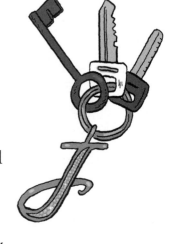

Outside, a horn honked and a bright red van pulled into the driveway.

"Dylan and Clara are back!" Jordan's face lit up in a grin and he raced out of the shed.

"Clara is Jordan's aunt, and Dylan is his cousin," Glitch explained. "They're here for the Maker Faire."

"I don't think I've ever seen Jordan smile that much before," Hajrah said.

Glitch laughed. "Yeah, well, Dylan is pretty cool. He knows a lot about electronics and robots."

We followed Jordan out of the shed and to the van. On the side, the words "Maker Masters" were painted in yellow letters. A lanky teenager opened the passenger door and climbed out. He had shaggy black hair and a hoodie with a skull on the front.

"Dylan!" Jordan high-fived his cousin and then turned to us. "These are my friends." Dylan gave us a quick wave. "Dylan and his mom drove in from Toronto last night and are staying with us."

Dylan's mom was as tall as her son and just as lanky.

"I'm Clara." She walked to the side of the van. "You must be Myron and Hajrah, the detectives looking for Jordan's runaway robot. Jordan's mom texted me about it earlier today."

"It didn't run away," I said. "It was stolen."

"Ah, yes, detectives must stick to the facts," she said. "Not as much fun that way, but it will help you find the robot."

Clara opened the van's side door and revealed several shelves holding containers bursting with wires, metal computer pieces, and much more.

Glitch rushed over, like a first grader in a toy store.

"Look at all these components," she said. "My brain is having a geek overload!"

"I know you don't have time to build a new robot for the maze competition, Glitch," Clara said. "But you're welcome to use any of our stuff if you just feel like building something."

"Thank you." Glitch couldn't take her eyes off all the computer parts.

"No problem. I always find that making

something helps me forget my troubles."
Clara ruffled Jordan's hair.

Hajrah peered into the van. "Why do you
have all this stuff?"

"Maker Masters is our family business."
Clara pointed to the words painted on the side
of the van. "We travel to Maker Faires and
show people how much fun it is to make stuff
with electronics—like Jordan and Glitch's
amazing robot."

"You saw Robson the Robot?" I asked.

"It was pretty impressive," Dylan said. "Glitch really knows her way around a circuit board. And Jordan's design was pretty sharp."

"It's a shame no one will ever see it in action," Clara said.

Hajrah popped her head up from a box of tiny colored lights. "Don't say that! We'll find Robson the Robot. We guarantee it! Don't we, Myron?"

Everyone looked at me. The back of my brain began to buzz. Detectives did not make guarantees. We told the truth. And the truth was we didn't know who took Robson the Robot.

Right now, the truth did not look good.

CHAPTER 5

Nate the Great was crumpled.

He didn't feel it. He was made of paper. Nate the Great is a character from one of my favorite detective series. He was also the latest entry in my *Mystery-o-pedia*, my encyclopedia of detectives from books. I have read all the Nate the Great books. He is the one who inspired me to look for mysteries in my neighborhood. But he's never had to look for missing robots.

It was Friday night. The Maker Faire started

tomorrow. The Robot Maze Challenge was on Sunday. We didn't have a lot of time to find Jordan and Glitch's robot. I needed to think. When I need to think, I work on my *Mystery-o-pedia*. My baby sister, Sofia, was asleep. Mom, Dad, and my older sister, Alicia, were watching TV in the living room. Thinking and TV don't go well together. So I was in the kitchen smoothing out a wrinkled detective, so I could glue him into the *Mystery-o-pedia*.

Questions wrinkled my brain, too. Who would steal a kid's robot? Jordan's shed was locked and the window painted shut, so how did the thief get in? Did Lionel take Jordan's robot plans? If not, then why were they taped to his maker-space table?

"Did you glue yourself to that chair, Myron?" Alicia stood in front of the fridge.

I hadn't heard her come into the kitchen.

"The glue isn't strong enough to stick me to the chair—oh," I said, looking up, "you were joking, weren't you?"

"Yes, little brother. I was joking. I know you don't like jokes."

"Yes I do," I said. "But only when they're funny."

"Ouch! That hurts," Alicia said, but she was smiling, so I knew she was still joking. She opened the fridge and took out a jug of homemade lemonade. "Working on another case?"

"Yes." I put the glue stick on the table and put the cap back on it.

"I bet a glass of lemonade would help you think." My sister knew me very well. She brought two glasses of lemonade to the table and sat down beside me. She looked at the pictures in my *Mystery-o-pedia*. "What's the latest case that has our great detective stumped?"

I sipped my lemonade and told her about Jordan and Glitch's robot and the Maker Faire. By the time I was done, Alicia had finished her drink.

"Sounds like you need to go to the Maker Faire tomorrow to do some investigating."

"That's my other problem," I said. "I don't have anyone to take me. Dad is working, and Mom is looking after Sofia. Hajrah's mom is working, too. We're stuck."

"No you're not," Alicia said. "I can take you."

"That would really help," I said.

"You're just lucky I promised Courtney I'd go with her. You can tag along." Alicia got up to go. She stopped at the door. "We're starting a movie. Want to join us? It's a mystery."

"I like mysteries."

"Really?" Alicia's eyes went wide. "I didn't know that about you."

"Yes you did!" I smiled. "Oh, you're joking again."

"Got you twice in one night, little brother."

Alicia laughed.

We went into the living room together. The movie was just starting. I had done enough thinking for one day.

A *Tyrannosaurus rex* towered over Oakdale Park.

It wasn't a real dinosaur. That would be impossible. This dinosaur was made out of old bicycle parts. It towered over the entrance to the park. Gears turned inside the dinosaur's body, making its head sway back and forth and its massive jaws open and shut. A sign hung across the path leading into the park. It read "Welcome to West Meadows Maker Faire."

The park was crowded. Families pushed strollers along the busy path, visiting booths that looked like little tents. Each booth had different gadgets on display. Adults and kids gathered around the booths, watching demonstrations or building their own mechanical creations. Music blasted from speakers on the far side of the park.

"This is going to be amazing!" Hajrah bounced up and down.

"It's going to be loud." I pulled a pair of earplugs out of my pocket and stuffed them into my ears. A good detective always comes prepared.

Beside us, Alicia checked her cell phone. "Okay, you two. Courtney is at the food vendors." She looked at the crowded park. "Are you sure you don't want to come with me?"

"We'll be fine on our own," I said. "Hajrah has her mom's phone. We can call you if anything happens."

"Okay." Alicia shrugged. "Stay together, and don't get lost."

"We're detectives," Hajrah said. "We don't get lost, we find lost things."

Alicia laughed. "Call me when you're ready to leave."

"You got it!" Hajrah stood at attention and saluted my sister.

Alicia walked through the bicycle dinosaur's legs and into the park. Hajrah spun around.

"Ready to find a robot?"

"We have other things to do first," I said, but she wasn't listening. She had already run past the dinosaur and was checking out the first booth. "And we're supposed to stick together." I grabbed a map of the Maker Faire from the welcome table and caught up to my runaway detective partner.

Even with my earplugs, the noise and people made my brain buzz. I don't like crowds. Coming here was a bad idea. But it was the only way we might find out who stole Robson the Robot.

A kid carrying a large cardboard box with "Maker Masters" printed on the side hurried toward us. "Coming through!" said a voice behind the box.

I stepped out of the way just in time to see who was being so pushy. Smasher McGintley stopped when she saw me.

"Myron the Snoop. What are you doing here?" she said with a snarl. "Where's Little

Miss Bounce-a-lot?"

"I'm right here!" Hajrah began jumping around Smasher, as if she had springs in her shoes. "What's in there? What have you got? Can I see?"

"None of your business!" Smasher growled. She guarded the box with her body.

"It looks pretty important." Hajrah bounced from one side of Smasher to the other.

"Go away!" Smasher snapped. "What's in here is none of your business."

"If it's Jordan and Glitch's robot, it is very much our business," I said.

Smasher laughed. "Maybe it *is* their robot in this box! Maybe I *am* the robot thief. But I'm not showing you what's inside. For a pair of detectives, you are totally clueless."

Smasher continued down the path. She was

still laughing as she pushed her way through the crowd and disappeared.

"Did Smasher just admit to being the robot thief?" Hajrah asked.

She had stopped bouncing and sounded confused. She wasn't alone. Whatever Smasher was up to, she was wrong about us. Hajrah and I had lots of clues. We just didn't know who stole the robot.

CHAPTER 6

We found the Maker Masters van near the
edge of the park.

The doors were open. Dylan was working
at one of tables beside the van. Clara sat
behind a table covered with gadgets. She was
too busy chatting with customers to notice us.

Dylan wore headphones and didn't hear
us coming.

"Hi, Dylan!" Hajrah said when she was
right beside him.

Dylan jumped at the sound of her voice and

pulled off his headphones.

"Hey, you guys. You startled me." He had a roll of duct tape in one hand and a small piece of metal in the other. The metal was flat, narrow, and about as long as my pinkie finger. One edge was jagged, with a little notch carved into it. The other edge was flat.

"What are you working on?" I asked.

"Nothing much." Dylan turned back to the table and began to clean up. "I was just messing around."

He slipped the metal into his pocket and put the duct tape away.

The smell of gasoline filled my nose. "Are you running a diesel engine?" I said.

"Nope, but they are." Dylan pointed to the bus station across the street from the park. A large bus drove out of the station and sent a plume of exhaust into the air. "I'm surprised you can smell that."

"Myron has a very good sense of smell," Hajrah said. "It's one of the reasons he's a great detective partner."

Clara joined us. "Hey, detectives. Any luck in your hunt for the missing robot?"

"Luck isn't necessary," I said. "Facts are all we need." Hajrah nudged me with her elbow. "But thanks for asking," I added.

"If it's facts you're after, I can tell you that Jordan and Glitch are at the maze challenge area," Clara said. "They're helping their teachers get set up for tomorrow's competition. The practice rounds are today." She checked her watch and glanced at Dylan. "Speaking of practice, shouldn't you be heading over there to get your robot set up?"

Dylan shrugged. "I'm ready to go."

"Really? I thought your robot wasn't working," Clara said.

"I fixed it," said Dylan. "No big deal."

"It sounded like a very big deal earlier this week. You complained about it all the way here. You said your bot was a lost cause, broken beyond repair."

Dylan scowled at his mom. "And now it's fixed. No. Big. Deal. Okay?"

"Okay." Clara looked confused. But then she smiled and ruffled Dylan's hair. "My son, the robot genius."

"Mom!" Dylan pushed her hand away. But he was also smiling. Maybe he didn't really mind her attention.

Clara's cell phone rang. "Better get this. Dylan can you watch the tables, please?"

We followed Dylan to the Maker Masters tables. Hajrah picked up a tiny yellow light from a box on the table.

"Pretty!" she said.

I was more interested in Dylan and his robot repairs. "I didn't know you had a bot in the maze challenge, too," I said.

"I almost didn't," Dylan said. "But I spent all morning fixing my bot, and now it's running perfectly."

"What's in those?" Hajrah pointed to a stack of boxes with the Maker Masters logo on them.

"Those are fully assembled mini-robots," Dylan said. "Mom puts them together, and we sell them ready to go out of the box."

"No assembly required?" Hajrah asked. "Doesn't that defeat the purpose of being a maker?"

"Don't blame us!" Dylan laughed. "Some people just want a robot. They don't want to actually build one."

Dylan's laugh faded as a teenager in ripped jeans came up to the table.

"Look, it's Dylan the Doofus!" The teen leaned on the table with his big hands. "I'm surprised you had the guts to show up here."

Dylan gave the new arrival a cold stare. "If it gives me a chance to wipe that smile off your face, Shane, then I wouldn't miss it."

"Whatever, Doofus," Shane said. "After all the bragging you did at the last Maker Faire, your robot is going to have to be pretty spectacular."

"Oh, I'll beat you, Shane," Dylan said. "My bot will run circles around your hunk of junk."

"If it can even finish the maze, that will be

a stretch for you." Shane gave us a withering look. "I'll leave you to hang out with your kindergarten friends. See you later, Doofus."

"What a creep," Hajrah said when he had gone.

"You got that right." Dylan sighed. "That's Shane Magwood. His family sells robot parts and travels with the Maker Faire, too. He thinks he's a robot genius just because he's won every maze challenge this year."

"And you told him you would win this race?" I asked.

Dylan nodded. "I was so mad last time, I couldn't help bragging that I would win. But it's not fair. Shane doesn't even build his own bots. His grandfather is an engineer and builds them for him."

"Is that allowed?" I asked.

"No, it's totally against the rules," Dylan said. "But Shane tells the judges he built the bot himself and they believe him."

"That's cheating!" Hajrah said.

"That's Shane," Dylan said, sighing again. A moment later, a smile spread across his face. "But I'll beat him tomorrow."

"I look forward to seeing that," I said.

The robot maze was at the back of the park. It was in a big open space and had barriers that went up to my knees. The barriers were the walls of the maze. When we arrived, three Maker Faire officials were moving the walls to create the twisty paths the bots were going to move through.

Off to one side of the maze, rows of worktables had been set up. At each table, a team of competitors worked on their robot, getting it ready for the big competition. We spotted Mr. Harpel and Ms. Fay at one, with the rest of the kids from West Meadows Elementary's Maker Club.

"Hajrah! Myron! Fancy meeting you here," Ms. Fay said when she saw us. "Have you come to cheer us on?"

"Our school bots don't compete until

tomorrow," Mr. Harpel said. "But you can watch our practice runs today."

"Robots need to practice?" Hajrah said.

"It's more for the programmers than the robots," Ms. Fay said. "They need to check that there are no mistakes in their computer code and that the robots can move through the maze."

Mr. Harpel pointed to the far end of the table. "Jordan and Glitch are down there. They've been here all morning helping the other kids with their robots."

"Are they really out of tomorrow's competition?" Hajrah asked.

"I'm afraid so," Ms. Fay said. "All teams had to have their bots registered by noon today or they can't compete tomorrow."

"So, even if we find Robson the Robot,

Jordan and Glitch are out of the maze competition." Hajrah looked at me. "Does that mean we give up?"

"Detectives don't give up," I said. "We haven't solved this mystery yet."

"I say we talk to Smasher again," Hajrah said. "We saw her earlier. She's up to something."

"I haven't seen her today." Mr. Harpel scratched his beard.

"Neither have I," Ms. Fay added. "But I could have missed her when she registered her bot."

Jordan and Glitch weren't happy to hear we hadn't found Robson yet.

"Our robot thief is somewhere out there," Jordan said. "And whoever took Robson is planning to run it in tomorrow's competition.

There's no other reason to take the robot—it's not worth much money."

"We've snooped around every table here but didn't see a robot with the same case," Glitch said.

"The thief could have tossed away the case. Right?" Hajrah said.

Glitch stood up. "That would be the best way to hide our bot's true identity."

"Or you could put it in a big box and not let anyone see it, like Smasher did," Jordan said in a growl. "I tried to get a look when she showed her bot to the judges. She nearly bit my head off."

"Why is Smasher acting so sneaky?" Hajrah asked.

Jordan pointed to a curly-headed kid on the far side of the maze. "And there's another sneak!"

"Lionel!" Hajrah said a little too loudly.

Lionel Aram looked up when he heard his name. He saw us and pushed his way into the crowd.

"It looks like he's not sick anymore," Hajrah said. "Where is he going?"

"Away from us," I said.

We raced around the tables, but by the time

we got to the other side of the maze, there was no sign of Lionel. Whatever he was up to, he definitely didn't want to talk to us about it.

"We'll never find him in this crowd," Hajrah said.

"Our number one suspect has got away from us twice," I said. "Next time, he won't be so lucky."

CHAPTER 7

The alley behind Jordan's house was much
quieter than the park. And smellier.

"Why are we here, Myron?" Hajrah stopped
walking. She plugged her nose with her
fingers. "It stinks."

Trash cans and bags of waste were stacked
outside carports. Garbage day must be soon.

"We need to take a close look at the scene of
the crime," I said.

"Didn't we do that? Jordan already showed
us the shed."

"Yes, but we want to know where the robot went after it was taken."

"Very logical, Mr. Detective!" Hajrah dropped her hand away from her nose and caught up with me.

"Help me search," I said. "We don't have much time."

The sun was already behind the trees. It would be dark soon.

We had met Alicia under the giant tyrannosaur. On the way home, questions nagged my brain. How did the thief get into the shed without breaking a window or damaging the lock? Where was Lionel, and why didn't he want to talk to us? And what was in Smasher's box?

Those questions wouldn't let us sit around the house. So Hajrah and I went out for a walk. And that walk led us here, to the alley behind Jordan's house. Hopefully, we'd find some answers among the trash.

I spotted the red shingles on the roof of Jordan's shed. A tall oak tree stretched up from the neighbor's yard and dangled its branches over the shed.

"Maybe the thief got in through the roof," Hajrah said when she saw me looking at the tree. "Climbed up the tree, went over the fence, and dropped right through."

I shook my head. "I don't think so. There weren't any holes in the roof."

Hajrah bounded onto a garbage can and then up onto the fence. She walked along it like a tightrope walker. "Still, we haven't actually had a close-up look at the roof." In three quick steps, she was on top of the shed.

"Be careful!" I called. Just watching her hop around the rooftop jumbled my stomach.

Hajrah scurried from one side of the roof to the other. She pulled on shingles and dangled her head over the edge, peering under the roof's overhang.

"This thing is pretty solid," she announced. "No signs of a loose shingle or a hole." She stood up and stared back down the alley. "Well, well, well. What do we have here?"

"What do we have where?" I spun around to look behind me. All I could see was a deserted alley with garbage ready to be collected.

90

Hajrah scampered down from the roof and landed like a cat pouncing on a mouse.

"Follow me," she said and ran across the alley.

She climbed onto a garbage bin and peered over a tall wooden fence.

"Gotcha!" she crowed.

"Got what?"

"Get up here and see for yourself."

"Um, I don't know." The bin was packed with garbage, and one wheel was missing. It wobbled under Hajrah's weight. "It doesn't look very safe."

Hajrah snorted. "Of course it's not safe, Myron. But it's the only way we'll solve the case. Now get up here!"

I climbed onto the bin and looked over the fence.

A brick path curved from the gate through

the backyard.
Chirping
chickadees hopped
from birdfeeders
swinging on poles
and branches.

"There!" she said.
"Do you see it?"

She pointed to a feeder with no birds at it.
It looked like an upturned box hanging from
four thin chains. It was made of plastic and
painted with red flames and skulls. It was
the strangest birdfeeder I had ever seen. And
that's because it wasn't a birdfeeder. It was the
clue we'd been looking for.

"Jordan's robot case!"

CHAPTER 8

"Get away from my birds!"

The voice came from the house. An old man in a blue sweater stomped into the yard.

And that's where we were standing.

"I told you we shouldn't hop over the fence," Hajrah said.

"You said we *should* hop over the fence!" I snapped.

"Okay. Then you *shouldn't* have listened to me."

With Jordan's robot case right there, we

couldn't resist going into the backyard for a closer look. And now the owner of the house was coming to get a closer look at us.

"What are you kids doing in my garden?" The old man squinted at us through his thick, black-rimmed glasses.

Hajrah stepped forward. "I'm Hajrah, and this is Myron. We are the West Meadows detectives." She stuck out her hand for the old man to shake. He just stared at it and blinked. Hajrah spun around to face me. "We should totally get business cards! Just like real detectives."

She spun back to the old man and pointed to the robot-case birdfeeder. "We were just admiring your amazing birdfeeder, sir! Such creativity. Very original."

"Thank you. I think." The old man nodded

to each of us. "I'm Sidney Cabot."

"Nice to meet you, Mr. Cabot!" Hajrah
danced around him. "We were curious to
know how you came up with the unique
designs on your birdfeeder."

Hajrah didn't stop moving. She bounced
away from the robot birdfeeder to a half-full
birdbath made out of an upturned hubcap
from a large truck, then skipped over to a set
of three colorful glass balls hanging from a
tree. She tapped each one, making them ding
like a musical instrument.

"Be careful with that, please," Mr. Cabot said.

"We're sorry for coming into your backyard," I said. "We're investigating a theft that happened around here recently."

Mr. Cabot turned at the sound of my voice. "A theft?" He adjusted his glasses so he could see me better. "What kind of theft?"

"A robot theft!" Hajrah said.

"It was a school project. It was taken from a shed near here." I pointed to Jordan's robot case hanging from a branch. "It looks just like this birdfeeder."

"That thing?" Mr. Cabot said. "I found that in my garbage this morning. No birds have come near it. I think the skulls scare them."

"All the hardware is gone," I said. "What happened to the wires and circuits?"

Mr. Cabot shrugged. "That's how I found it. It was just sitting in my garbage. I figured it was a box for some kind of toy."

"Did you see who put it in your garbage?" I asked.

"When I took out some trash last night before going to bed, it wasn't there. When I went out early this morning, there it was."

"So it must have happened late at night," I said.

Mr. Cabot shrugged. "If you say so, detective."

"Could we take it and return it to our friend? He'll be happy to have it back."

"Sure. I don't want stolen property in my backyard." Mr. Cabot took the robot case off the branch and emptied the seeds out of it. "The birds sure won't miss it."

"I guess they don't like stolen birdfeeders," I said.

The old man handed me the case. "I think you're right."

I turned to Hajrah. She was staring up at the house.

"Let's go tell Jordan we found part of his stolen robot."

"Let's tell him we found the robot thief, too." She pointed to an attic window.

I looked up in time to see someone with dark, curly hair duck away from the window. The curtains swung back into place. I didn't get a good look, but I had seen enough.

We had found Lionel.

CHAPTER 9

I sipped my hot chocolate and watched
Lionel squirm.

He sat across from me at the kitchen table.
Jordan's robot case was in the middle of
the table. Hajrah sat beside me, poking the
marshmallows floating in her hot chocolate
with her finger.

"Three pinks!" She blew at the steam rising
up from her mug. "That means I'm lucky."

Mr. Cabot put a mug of hot chocolate in
front of Lionel. Lionel didn't take his eyes off

the robot case.

After we spotted Lionel at the window, we explained to Mr. Cabot about the design plans we found at Lionel's maker-space table. That was enough for Mr. Cabot to invite us in for a chat with his grandson.

Mr. Cabot joined us at the table with his own mug of hot chocolate.

"Okay, kids, I called your parents to let them know you're here," he said. "Myron, your mom will be here soon to take you both home."

"Thank you," I said.

Mr. Cabot turned to his grandson. "Okay, Lionel, want to tell us what's going on?"

"I was going to say that," I said. They all looked at me. "As the detective here, I'm supposed to ask the questions."

"I apologize, Myron." Mr. Cabot chuckled. "Please proceed."

I turned to our number one suspect. "Why were Jordan's robot plans stuck to the bottom of your maker-space table?"

Lionel looked into his hot chocolate. Maybe he was thinking. Maybe he was counting marshmallows.

"I took them," he said eventually.

"Aha!" Hajrah jumped to her feet and pointed dramatically at Lionel. "You *are* the robot thief!"

"No!" Lionel's eyes were wide with panic. "I didn't steal the robot. Just the plans. Honest."

"Oh." Hajrah flopped back into her chair. "Then I'm confused."

I sipped my drink. "So am I."

Lionel sighed. "It started last week. Everyone in the Maker Club was making a robot for the maze challenge. Glitch promised she would help me with mine. But then she was too busy building her own bot."

"Didn't your teacher help?" Mr. Cabot asked.

"Ms. Fay is really smart, but she doesn't know everything about computer code. She always says that she is just there to guide us on our journey of discovery." Lionel scowled at his hot chocolate. "Whatever that means."

Hajrah poked the floating marshmallows with her finger again. "Yeah, she says stuff like that to me, too."

"I was really mad at Glitch," Lionel said. "I took the robot plans to get back at her. Without those plans, I figured she would make a mistake and her robot wouldn't work.

She'd be stuck."

"Just like you were stuck?" Hajrah said. She didn't look up from the marshmallows.

"I taped the plans under my table," Lionel said. "I was going to give them back when Glitch apologized for not helping me. But when I got to school yesterday, I heard their robot was stolen. I knew if I admitted to taking the plans, everyone would think I took the robot, too."

"You pretended to be sick so you could leave school early," I said.

"You told me you were on death's door." Mr. Cabot glared at his grandson through his thick glasses.

"I'm sorry, Grandpa," he said. "You have to believe me. I didn't take the robot, but I saw the person who did."

I sat up straight. "Go on."

"I didn't see much. It was dark. I was in bed. My room looks over the back alley. I heard the garbage lid shut and thought it was the raccoons again."

"Raccoons," Mr. Cabot said in a growl. "They're always getting into the garbage and making a mess."

"But it wasn't raccoons?" Hajrah said.

"Nope." Lionel took another sip of hot chocolate. "When I went to the window to look, all I saw was a person walking up the alley, toward Jordan's house."

"You didn't actually see this person with the robot?" I asked.

"No, but there was no one else around," Lionel said. "It was dark. They wore a hoodie. I didn't see what the person looked like.

I don't even know if it was a boy or a girl."

We were all silent for a moment. Suddenly, Lionel pushed back his chair.

"Be right back," he said, and he ran out of the kitchen.

His feet thumped up the stairs.

"Sounds like he's going to his room," Mr. Cabot said.

Forty-five seconds later, Lionel came back into the kitchen.

"When Grandpa found the robot case, he brought it into the kitchen. I recognized it right away, but I didn't say anything." Lionel put a piece of orange plastic on the table. "This was lying inside. It looked like the last candy in a bowl, so I took it."

The piece of plastic was almost as long as my thumb and round, like a cylinder. It had red paint on one end, but the rest of it was orange. Something had split the plastic down the middle, so it could open and close like a mouth.

"It's broken," I said. "It looks like it's been stepped on by something heavy."

"That's how I found it," Lionel said quickly. "I have no idea what it is."

Hajrah leaned across the table to get a closer look at the piece of cracked plastic.

"Another clue!" she said. "Thanks, Lionel."

I didn't share my partner's excitement. I didn't know why, but something about our new clue didn't feel right. Before I could ask another question, the doorbell rang.

"That'll be your mom, Myron." Mr. Cabot got up from his chair. "Visit us another time, so we can chat again."

"This wasn't a chat," I said. "It was an interview, and we're not finished."

"Well, we don't want to keep your mom waiting." Mr. Cabot smiled. "You can finish your interview with Lionel at school on Monday."

Mr. Cabot left the kitchen to answer the door. Hajrah took the robot case from the table. Lionel collected the mugs and took them to the sink.

"I hope you find the thief," he said.

"We will, Lionel." I put the piece of plastic in my pocket. "Detectives don't stop until they've uncovered the truth."

Hajrah sat next to me in the backseat as my

mom drove us home. She was picking at the piece of plastic Lionel had given us.

"Myron!" she said suddenly. "There's a number on this thing!"

She held it up for me to see. The number "37" was etched into one end of the plastic cylinder.

"It was covered by a bit of red paint." Hajrah bounced in her seat.

"What does it mean?" I asked. "And why was it painted over?"

"No idea, but I'm sure it will lead us to Robson the Robot." Hajrah beamed. "This is our lucky clue."

"Detectives don't need luck," I grumbled. "We don't even know if Lionel is telling the truth. He could be hiding the rest of the robot somewhere. And we don't even know what that thing is. It could be a red herring. You know—a fake clue to throw the detectives off the trail of the thief."

Hajrah rolled her eyes. "I know what a red herring is, Myron. I just think you're wrong. It *is* a lucky clue."

My mom pulled the car into Hajrah's driveway. Hajrah said good-bye and got out. Before she closed the door, she turned back to me. "Myron, just like a good detective needs a partner, a good detective also needs a little luck." She handed me the piece of plastic. It was warm. "See you tomorrow, partner."

I put the plastic in the robot case. It sat in my lap the rest of the way home. Lionel was right. The plastic did look like the last candy in a bowl. I wished the bowl would fill up with answers, but when we got home, I still had only questions.

Did Lionel really see someone in the alley last night? Or was he making that up to hide the fact that he stole the bot? Where did the piece of orange plastic come from? Did he really find it with the robot case, or was he making that up, too?

I didn't know if we could trust Lionel. He had taken the robot plans. He had lied to his grandfather and the school about being sick. And he had run away from us at the park.

Maybe he was making up this story about a kid in a hoodie to throw us off the trail.

Lionel lived down the alley from Jordan. He could have snuck out at night, taken the robot, and been back in bed before anyone noticed. But how did he get into the shed? I couldn't answer that question yet. But until I had my hands on all of Robson the Robot, Lionel was still a suspect.

And then there was Smasher. No one had seen her robot. Jordan said she didn't do any building at the maker space. And her house is at the top of Jordan's street and has access to the back alley, too. My brain buzzed just thinking about it.

I opened my notebook and drew straight lines and squares until I had a map of Jordan's back alley.

I looked at the picture until my mom told me to turn my light out. As I drifted off to sleep, one question floated through my mind: Why was the robot thief walking *toward* Jordan's shed?

CHAPTER 10

The early morning sun climbed over the trees lining Jordan's street. Hajrah and I stood on his doorstep, waiting.

"Where is he?" I said. "Jordan knows we're coming. I called him as soon as I woke up."

"You called me, too, remember?" Hajrah yawned. "You totally ruined my Sunday morning sleep-in."

"We don't have time to sleep," I said. "We need to catch the robot thief before the maze challenge begins later today."

Jordan opened the door. He wore pajamas with little spaceships all over. Each spaceship was red and white and had a green alien riding it like a surfboard. His pajamas didn't make sense. Why would an alien ride a spaceship like a surfboard? An alien would be inside the spaceship.

Jordan's eyes went wide at the sight of the robot case in my hands.

"Robson!"

"Part of Robson," Hajrah clarified.

"It's just the case," I said. "But don't worry. We'll find the rest of your robot."

Jordan hugged the robot case like it was a lost puppy that had come home.

"Why is there birdseed in it?"

"Long story. I thought I cleaned it all out," Hajrah said.

"It's okay. I'm just happy to have part of Robson back." Jordan led us into the kitchen. "My parents are still asleep. Dylan and Clara are upstairs, getting ready to leave for the Maker Faire."

Through the kitchen window, I saw Glitch open the back gate and wheel her bike into the backyard.

"Hooray! We're all here," Hajrah said.

"Let's talk in the shed," I said.

Jordan led us to the back door. Coats hung from a row of hooks on the wall. A small potted plant sat on the windowsill.

"Grab my keys, Myron, and let everyone into the shed," said Jordan. "I'll change and meet you there."

Jordan's key chain with the fancy "J" hung on a small hook by the window. I grabbed it and hurried out the door.

Once we were all in the shed, Glitch examined the robot case. She wasn't happy. "The thief just yanked the case off. The edge is bent, and the paint is chipped," she said. Glitch peeled off a bit of red paint from the painted flames on the side of the case. "See?"

"Red paint!" Hajrah squealed. "Just like the bit stuck to the lucky clue."

"What lucky clue?" Jordan asked.

"This." I held up the piece of plastic. "Hajrah found red paint on it."

"Do you think the paint came from Robson the Robot?" Jordan said.

"Maybe," Hajrah said. "But we don't even know what the thing is."

Glitch took the piece of plastic and pulled her laptop from her bag. "Give me five minutes and I can find out."

Four minutes and thirty-six seconds later, Glitch looked up from the laptop.

"It's a key." She grinned.

"It doesn't look like a key." Hajrah studied the cracked cylinder lying on the worktable. "It's too small and too orange."

"That's because it's just the handle of the key," Glitch said.

Her laptop screen showed a website for a key company, with a photograph of a metal key with an orange plastic cylinder stuck on one end. The plastic looked exactly like the lucky clue.

"It's a locker key. People store their stuff and lock it up with this." She pointed to the photo of the metal piece sticking out of the plastic. "Someone broke this bit off."

The bit was narrow with a jagged notch carved in one side. I couldn't see the other side of the metal, but I knew it would be flat. I had seen a piece of metal like this before somewhere.

"It's probably an old key, because the plastic is pretty brittle," Glitch continued. "That would make it break easily. It could be for a locker at a pool or an amusement park."

"Or a bus station," I said. The lucky clue was beginning to make sense.

"There's a bus station across the street from Oakdale Park!" Hajrah said. "You smelled the diesel fuel."

"I did. Inside that station are lockers." I picked up the piece of plastic and held it so everyone could see the numbers. "And inside locker number 37 is Robson the Robot."

Jordan jumped to his feet. "We have to open that locker!"

"How?" Glitch said. "We don't have the key. We just have the handle. We'll never be able to open it."

I heard the back doors of the Maker Masters van slam shut outside. I remembered where I had seen that piece of metal before.

"We don't need to open the locker," I said.

"The robot thief will do it for us."

Clara came out of the house and walked to the Maker Masters van. Dylan was already waiting at the passenger door.

"Myron, can you get out of the way, please? We have to leave for the park."

I was standing in the middle of the driveway. It was part of my plan. It wasn't a good plan, but I didn't have time for a good plan.

"I solved the case," I said.

"That's nice." Clara smiled.

"I know who stole Jordan's robot."

Clara's eyebrows went up. They stayed up. "Who was it?"

Jordan arrived from the shed, carrying

Robson the Robot's case. Glitch and Hajrah followed him. Dylan's mouth fell open as his cousin walked past.

Nobody spoke. That was also part of my plan.

Clara opened the van door. "We don't have time for guessing games, kids. I'm glad you found the robot, but we need to get to the Maker Faire."

Dylan stood completely still. He glared at the robot case as if it were his worst enemy. Then his shoulders slouched and his gaze dropped to the ground.

"It was me," Dylan mumbled.

"What?" Clara said.

"I took Jordan's robot." Dylan's voice cracked as he spoke.

"You've got a van full of robots," Glitch said. "Why steal ours?"

"Because your robot was the best Dylan had ever seen," I said.

"Dylan bragged to Shane Magwood that he could build a robot that would win the competition." Hajrah looked straight at Dylan. "But you knew you couldn't do it."

"I'm not that good at writing computer code," Dylan said. "My robot was a disaster. It wouldn't even move properly."

"You were going to lose the maze competition," I said. "Shane Magwood would never let you forget it. You were panicking. Then you arrived in West Meadows and saw Jordan and Glitch's robot."

"It worked perfectly." Dylan looked at the ground. "It was exactly what I needed to beat Shane."

"So you just took it?" Jordan asked.

Dylan didn't answer.

"You got up early Friday morning, before anyone else, and snuck into the shed," I said. "You took the robot, put it in the van, and went to the park with your mom to set up for the weekend. You couldn't keep it in the van because your mom might find it. So you hid it in a locker at the bus station."

"But at the bus station, you realized someone would recognize Jordan's artwork. So you had to get rid of the case," Hajrah said. "You didn't have your tools, so you used the locker key to pry the case off. That's how you got red paint on it."

"But the key snapped and you panicked," I said. "You didn't have much time. You had to get back and help your mom. You hid the robot in the locker, stuffed the case into your backpack, and hurried back to the park."

"But you still had a problem," I went on. "You had to get the robot out of the locker on Saturday. You were trying to make a new handle for the key when I saw you yesterday."

Hajrah bounced on the spot as she spoke. "You had to get rid of the robot case. At the end of the day, you brought it back here and dumped it in a garbage can in the alley. You remembered you still had the plastic from the key, so you tossed that in there, too. That's why Lionel saw you walking toward Jordan's place after you ditched the robot case."

"That one had me confused," I said. "Why would a thief take something and then go right back to the scene of the crime? Then I realized the scene of the crime was where the thief was spending the night."

"And you were able to get into the shed in the first place," Hajrah said, "because the key hung next to Jordan's back door. Only someone staying in the house would be able to get it."

"That ruled out Lionel and Smasher," I said. "But now there was another suspect."

"Me." Dylan spoke so quietly we could barely hear him. "It's all true. I took the key, went into the shed, and stole your robot. I dumped the shell so no one would see it and recognize it. I'm sorry."

The others were silent. Everyone looked sad. We had solved the case, but I didn't feel happy.

CHAPTER 11

The key fit locker 37 perfectly.

"Robson!" Jordan gently lifted the robot out of the bus station locker. He turned to Dylan. "Does it still work?"

Dylan nodded quickly. "It works perfectly. I wouldn't damage it, little cousin."

"Don't call me that," Jordan snapped. "Glitch and I are out of the maze challenge because of you. That's not what families do. You are *not* my cousin anymore!"

Glitch glared at Dylan, then began to inspect

the robot.

Dylan slumped against the locker. Beside us, Clara hung up her cell phone.

"Did it work?" Hajrah bounced and tugged on her braid.

Clara grinned. "Jordan and Glitch, get Robson ready to race. You're back in the maze challenge."

The two friends looked up.

"I don't understand," Jordan said.

"How did you get us into the competition?" Glitch asked.

"I spoke to the judges and told them what Dylan did. I asked them to let you race Robson in his place," Clara said. "You can thank Myron and Hajrah. It was their idea."

"It was the most logical solution," I said. "The judges had already approved Robson to be in the competition."

I had never seen Glitch smile so much.

"Thanks, you guys," she said. She carefully snapped Robson's case into place.

"You're very welcome." Hajrah bowed like she was the star of the school play. "We're the West Meadows detectives. Solving mysteries is what we do!"

"And winning the robot maze challenge is

what *we're* going to do," Jordan said.

Clara laughed and looked at her watch. "We should hurry. The challenge begins soon."

Jordan picked up Robson and faced his cousin.

"I'm still mad at what you did," Jordan said. "But you can watch us race if you want."

"Thanks," Dylan said in a quiet voice. "I'd like that."

Clara led us out of the bus station. She spoke quietly with Dylan as we crossed the street into the park. I didn't have to hear them to know they were talking about what he did. When we got to the Maker Faire, Clara hugged him. Dylan was still in trouble, but he was going to be okay.

Jordan and Glitch were more than okay. They ran to the robot maze, chatting excitedly.

DEPARTURES

"Look how happy they are." Hajrah twirled around, her arms held out wide. "We made that happen. Thanks to our amazing mystery-solving skills!"

I pulled the piece of orange plastic from my pocket and showed it to my detective partner. "Our amazing skills. And a little bit of luck."

Liked this book?
Join Myron and friends
as they crack another case!

On Myron's first day at a new school the kitchen is burgled and the snacks go missing! Together with Hajrah and Glitch, Myron gets to the bottom of the mystery—all while keeping bully Sarah "Smasher" McGintley off their trail.

> **❝** I like this book because it has fun pictures and it is a mystery…Myron and Hajrah make a good team. **❞**
> — **Rachel, age 9**